THE NOGRE

BY DICK CLEMENT

ILLUSTRATED BY
CHRISTOPHER WHITTLE

C000137839

To Philippa,
I'm told 'Nogres
Listen for Publishers
who never say
'Yes'!

Christopher
Whittle

January 17th 2023

© Dick Clement, 2021

All rights reserved. No part of this book may be reproduced or utilized in any form or by any means, electronic or mechanical, including photocopying, recording, or by any information storage and retrieval system, without permission in writing from the author.

First published in 2021

Written by Dick Clement
Illustrated by Christopher Whittle (FatSquirrelStudios.com)
Interior page design by Bryony van der Merwe
Special thanks to Dennis Dugan

ISBN: 978-1-7923-8113-3 (paperback edition)
ISBN: 978-1-7923-8167-6 (hardcover edition)
ISBN: 978-1-7923-8114-0 (electronic edition)

Dedication

To my grandchildren,
especially the one
who used to say
'No' a lot.

Eliza, Ella, Felix, Jules,
Oscar, Rafe, Rowan
and Stanley.

We've all heard of Ogres and they're **very scary**

UGLY and **LUMPY** and **NASTY** and **HAIRY**

But there's something **much worse** than your average **Ogre.**

Just hope that you **NEVER** bump into...

Nogres listen for children who never say 'Yes',

Which causes their families a great deal of stress.

Whatever the question, they always decline
Sometimes with a *pout,*
sometimes with a *whine,*
Sometimes with a *stamp*
of a foot or a *shout*

So that passing-by
strangers say:

WHAT'S
THAT
ABOUT?

One particular boy had a 'NO' in his name
Namely, Noah Harbottle, who thought it a game

To say
'NO!'
to his bath time

and
'NO!'
to his bed

And
'NO!'
to pyjamas
going over his head.

Or maybe the chimney or straight
through the wall –
Locks and bolts don't present
any problem at all.

His teeth are coal black and
his nose cherry red
Dogs and cats hear his voice and
hide under the bed!'

'That's only the half of it, Noah', said Dad.

'I've heard that he smells like a
fish that's gone bad.

Just say
one more word
and he'll visit for sure!'

'NO
HE WON'T!'
yelled the boy,
as they walked out the door.

He was quiet for a while, alone in his bed.
'No such thing as a Nogre',
he said in his head.

Then he heard something stir
in the darkness outside
And he mumbled 'Who's there?'
and though nothing replied

He smelt something rotten *brought in on the wind*

And something appeared and the

AWFUL THING GRINNED.

'NO!' stuttered Noah,
with no way of knowing
That this final 'NO' was
the key to get going.

He was seized by a hand that was DRIPPING WITH SLIME...

And they started a journey **through SPACE** and *through TIME*

It was night, it was day,

THEY WERE UP, THEY WERE DOWN

Till they came down to earth in an odd kind of town.
The traffic lights blinked,
every one of them red.
NO people, NO cars,
only street signs instead.

'There are rules', said the Nogre, 'I chose to impose.
Some things are Forbidden
and others are no-nos.

For anything here
that you might want to do
You'll find a sign somewhere that says it's taboo.'

'PRIVATE! NO ENTRY!'
read a sign on a door.

The Nogre pushed through it,
then opened one more
That read
'NO ADMITTANCE'.

Inside was a hall

Full of children like Noah,
not happy at all.

The Nogre explained: 'They are all just like you
They said 'NO' once too often – come meet one or two.'

They all spoke at once:

'I said 'No' to my mother.
'My Grandma',
'My Uncle',
'My Sister',
'My Brother.'

'I said **'NO'** to my dinner', a sad-faced boy said.
'I'd eaten four donuts and chocolate instead.'

'I had a big fight over watching TV'
Said a girl, 'Now it doesn't seem worth it to me.'

Noah heard all their stories and they made him sad
To think of the times he'd made Mum and Dad mad.

Sometimes he said 'NO'
just because he was bored
And sometimes he felt
he was being ignored.

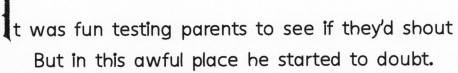

It was fun testing parents to see if they'd shout
But in this awful place he started to doubt.

Perhaps it was not the best way to behave

So he took a deep breath and he tried to be

BRAVE.

He looked at the children, so lonely and sad.
  'Do you want to go home?
    To your Mum and your Dad?'

They nodded their heads. 'Okay, here's what we'll do.
We'll say our last 'No' to the Nogre.
WE'RE THROUGH!'

Then he laughed, with a
GURGLING,
TERRIBLE SOUND,

It scared Noah stiff,
but he still held his ground.

He turned to the others and lifted his voice

'If we **all** stand together, we still *have a choice.*

There's one magic word we can use - *can you guess?'*

Their faces lit up and they all shouted:

The Nogre went pale,
so they said it once more.

And he started to shrink,
so they made for the door.

Noah whirled through the air
and he heard a great

BOOM

When he opened his eyes,
he was back in his room!

His mother looked in and said
'Are you okay?'

'Oh, the Nogre dropped in
but I scared him away.

Though from now on I'm going to say 'No' a lot less.

The word I'll be
using more often is
'YES'.

Now breaking bad habits is quite hard to do

But Noah's developed A NEW POINT OF VIEW

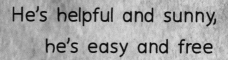

He's helpful and sunny,
he's easy and free

And most people find
he's inclined to agree

He'll say **'NO'** on occasions –
to some things you should.
Or he'll answer politely:
'Well maybe I could.'

And there's peace in the Harbottle family at last

Now that Noah's No-saying's a thing of the past.

purrrr

ABOUT THE AUTHOR

Dick Clement has enjoyed a long and successful career in television, movies and theatre. In partnership with Ian La Frenais their British TV series include *Porridge, Whatever Happened to the Likely Lads* and *Auf Wiedersehen, Pet.* Films include *The Commitments, Flushed Away* and *Across the Universe.* Their dual memoir, *More Than Likely,* was published by Weidenfeld and Nicolson two years ago.

Printed in Great Britain
by Amazon

16674383R00027